An I Can Read Book®

BINKY BROTHERS, DETECTIVES

by JAMES LAWRENCE

Pictures by
LEONARD KESSLER

HARPER & ROW, PUBLISHERS

BINKY BROTHERS, DETECTIVES
Text copyright © 1968 by J. D. Lawrence
Illustrations copyright © 1968 by Leonard Kessler
Printed in the United States of America for Harper & Row, Publishers, Inc.
Library of Congress Catalog Card Number: 68–10374
ISBN 0-06-023759-7 (lib. bdg.)

BINKY BROTHERS, DETECTIVES

"That sign is a mess,"

said Albert Binky.

"Can't you even spell right?"

"Who cares?" said Dinky.

"Everyone will know what I mean."

Dinky was Albert's little brother.

His real name was Norbert.

But he was so little

everyone called him Dinky.

Dinky Binky.

"Now what are you doing?"

asked Albert.

"Printing my name," said Dinky.

"Like fun you are!" said Albert.

"I thought up this detective stuff,

so my name goes first.

You are just my helper."

Albert had red hair,

so everyone called him Pinky.

Pinky Binky.

Dinky made a face.

"You always want to be boss,"

he said.

"Never mind that," said Pinky.

"Mom made the lemonade for us.

If you want to help out

at the stand, come on."

"That reminds me," said Dinky.

"Did Patsy Ann ever pay us

for finding her turtle?"

"Sure," said Pinky.

"I forgot to tell you.

Here is your share."

He gave Dinky a nickel.

"Where is the rest?" asked Dinky.

Pinky looked down

at his little brother.

"What do you mean

where is the rest?"

"Well," said Dinky,

"you told Patsy Ann

it would cost twenty cents.

Half of twenty is ten.

Besides, I found her turtle."

"Look," said Pinky,

"you are just my helper.

So you get five."

LEMONADE 2¢

They did not sell much lemonade.

Finally Chub Doolin came along.

"Hot dog!" said Pinky.

"Here comes lots of business!"

Chub could eat more
and drink more
than any three kids
on the block.

He looked upset.

"Someone swiped my

catcher's mitt," he said.

This was bad news.

Pinky had to pitch

a big baseball game

after lunch.

Chub was his catcher.

Their team was playing

the Elm Street Wildcats.

"How do you know

someone took your mitt?"

Pinky asked.

"It was hanging on a nail

in our garage," said Chub.

"Now it is gone.

This note was on the nail."

He took out a piece of pink paper.

Ha Ha! I
have your
mitt. Now
the wildcats
will beat you.
Guess who?

"What are we going to do?"

said Chub.

"I have a glove you can use,"

said Dinky, "if you let me play."

"Are you kidding?" said Chub.

"Your brother throws hard.

I cannot catch his stuff

with your skinny little glove."

18

"Never mind him, Chub,"
said Pinky.

"Just leave the note with me.

I will get to work

on this case right away."

"Okay," said Chub.

He drank four lemonades

and left.

"What are you
going to do, Pink?"
asked Dinky.

"Don't rush me," said Pinky.

"I will think of something."

Spike Brown and Joe Parker

came up to the stand.

They were Wildcats.

They liked to act smart.

"Hi, Pink," said Spike.

"How is your pitching arm?"

"You will find out," said Pinky.

"Don't worry, Pink," said Joe.

"If we hit too many homers,

you can let your kid brother

pitch for you."

That made Pinky mad.

"Maybe I will," he said.

"Even Dinky could beat you guys."

Spike and Joe laughed.

They each had a lemonade.

"Don't worry about Chub either,"

said Spike.

"We will get so many hits,

he will hardly need a glove."

Spike took out his money to pay.

Something fell out of his pocket.

A piece of pink paper.

Dinky opened his mouth

to say something.

Pinky stepped on his foot,

hard.

"Come on, Joe," said Spike.

Dinky held his foot.

"What's the big idea?"

he said. "That hurt."

"You are supposed to be

a detective," said Pinky.

"I know," said Dinky.

"I just wanted to ask Spike

how come he knew about Chub's mitt."

"Maybe he is the one

who took it," said Pinky.

"Ever think of that?"

He picked up the paper.

It was the same kind

of pink paper

as Chub's note!

"See what I mean?" said Pinky.

"This could be a clue."

"Wow!" yelled Pinky.

"It's a clue all right!"

Mel was Melvin Krantz,

the Wildcat shortstop.

"What does it mean?"

asked Dinky.

"Don't you get it?" said Pinky.

"Mel must be the one

who took Chub's mitt.

If Chub has no mitt,

I cannot pitch so hard.

Then they can win the game."

Dinky's mouth dropped open.

He was trying hard

to figure things out.

"What does he mean

about looking high enough?"

Dinky asked.

"Did he hide the mitt

in his attic?"

31

"No," said Pinky.

"The house he hid it in

does not have an attic.

It is not that kind of house."

"What kind is it?" said Dinky.

Pinky smiled.

"The kind a monkey

could climb up to—in a tree."

"But," said Dinky,

"why did Spike . . . ?"

Pinky did not let him finish.

He just patted Dinky.

"Forget it," he said.

"You watch the stand.

I have things to do."

"Okay," said Dinky.

"If we find Chub's mitt,

can I play?"

"What do you mean

if *we* find it?" said Pinky.

Then he hurried off

to the Wildcat tree house.

The tree house was in the woods

back of Elm Street.

A ladder was leaning

against the tree.

Pinky looked all around.

No Wildcats in sight.

Pinky climbed the ladder.

He was chuckling to himself.

How surprised the Wildcats would be!

The note said Chub and his pals

would never look high enough

unless one of them was a monkey.

Ha ha, thought Pinky.

I will fool those wise guys!

Then he heard someone laugh.

Pinky looked down.

There were Spike and Joe!

They pulled down the ladder.

"Have fun up there,

you monkey!" Spike yelled.

They ran off, laughing.

Pinky just sat there,

feeling dumb.

The tree trunk was too big

to slide down.

Pinky hated to call for help.

But what else could he do?

So he yelled.

And hollered.

It was no use.

The wood lot was too big

for anyone to hear him.

What a mess! Pinky thought.

How could his team

beat the Wildcats

without their number one pitcher?

All of a sudden

a voice called,

"Hey, Pinky!"

There was Dinky

coming through the bushes.

Pinky felt like hugging him.

"Dinky! Set that ladder up for me."

"Sure, Pink,"

said his little brother,

"but first we got some things

to talk over."

"What do you mean

we have things to talk over?"

Pinky asked.

44

"Like about finding

Chub's mitt," said Dinky.

Pinky had forgotten

all about the mitt.

"Wait a second," he said.

"I will see if it is here."

"Don't bother," said Dinky.

"I already found it."

Pinky stared at his little brother.

"Where was it?" he asked.

"On a nail in Chub's garage,"
said Dinky.

"But Chub told us
it was gone," said Pinky.

"It was," said Dinky.

"But I was pretty sure
the Wildcats would put it back.
I mean after you fell
for their trick."

Pinky felt his face getting red.

"The note was just a trick?"

he asked.

"Sure," said Dinky.

"I tried to tell you,

but you would not listen."

"I am listening," said Pinky.

"Go ahead and tell me now."

"Spike likes to play tricks,"

said Dinky.

"He dropped the note on purpose.

Besides, that monkey stuff

sounded like a joke."

"Gee whiz, I never thought of that,"

said Pinky.

"It was easy

for a good detective," said Dinky.

Pinky hated to say it

but he did.

"Okay," he said. "You win.

Now set up the ladder."

But Dinky shook his head.

"Not yet, Pink.

We still got things to talk over."

Pinky gritted his teeth.

"What do you want?" he asked.

"Can I play a couple of innings?"
said Dinky.

"Now look," said Pinky.

"You are not good enough

to play the Wildcats."

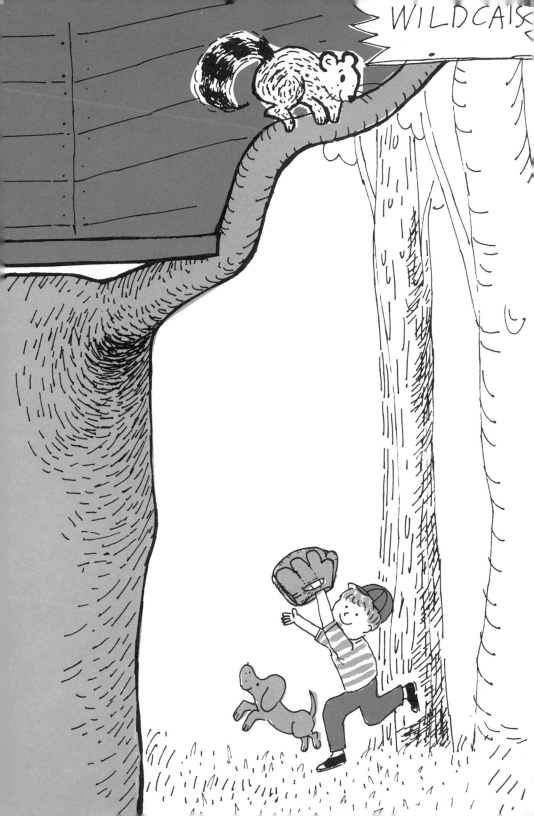

Dinky did not say a word.

He started to walk away.

"Okay, okay!" Pinky hollered.

"You can play."

Dinky turned around.

"How much do I get

for finding Patsy Ann's turtle?"

he asked.

"So we are partners," said Pinky.

"We will split fifty-fifty.

You get ten cents."

"Nothing doing," said Dinky.

"I want the whole twenty cents."

Pinky did not like it,

but he had to give in.

Dinky made him

throw down the money.

Then he set up the ladder.

Pinky was boiling mad.

Some partner! he thought.

Still, it was better

than staying up

in that tree all day.

So Pinky was able to pitch

for his team

after all.

Of course,

they had to let Dinky

play awhile.

They beat the Wildcats anyhow.

Later, Pinky got another surprise.

"Hi, partner!" said Dinky.